THE BIRD family live in the grounds of BONC – the National Bureau of Clever Experts, where some very odd experiments go on. Mr Bird installs a safety and protection system to take care of his family. When Mrs Bird inadvertently activates the system, the kitchen takes off into space with Mrs Bird and the children in it. After a series of adventures, Mr Bird joins them in space, having put the garden shed into orbit to do so, and together they deal with a succession of aliens and space monsters.

A is for Aaargh!
The Bunk-Bed Bus
The Summertime Christmas Present
Who's Afraid of the Ghost Train?

Frank Rodgers

The Intergalactic Kitchen

BARN OWL BOOKS

First published in Great Britain 1990 by Viking
This edition first published 2001 by Barn Owl Books
157 Fortis Green Road, London N10 3LX
Barn Owl Books are distributed by Frances Lincoln

ISBN I 903015 I2 X

A CIP catalogue record for this book is available
from the British Library

Designed by Douglas Martin
Printed in China

This is Mr and Mrs Bird.

Mr Bird works at the National Bureau of Clever Experts. (NBOCE. But the clever experts call it BONCE because clever people like anagrams.)

Mr Bird is clever but very absent-minded.

Mrs Bird is clever too. She works part time at the local library.

She also works at home looking after their old house and their four children . . .

6

The Bird house stands in the backyard of BONCE, the National Bureau of Clever Experts (Space Exploration Section).

Mr Bird needs to be close to his work because he is the janitor.

So, while he looks after this building, Mrs Bird looks after their own.

THE BIRD HOUSE

BONCE

KITCHEN EXTENSION

GARDEN SHED.

Mr and Mrs Bird built the kitchen extension and garden shed themselves. Nice, aren't they?

Mr Bird knows that the work that the clever experts do at BONCE is HIGHLY SECRET (Shhh!) and PROBABLY DANGEROUS.

So, one week, while the rest of the family were visiting Auntie Mabel, he set to work in the kitchen . . .

. . . and installed a highly secret (and probably dangerous) safety and protection system for the family to use in an emergency.

So far, they haven't needed to use it – which is probably just as well because, being absent-minded (he must have caught it from the clever experts), he forgot to tell Emily (Mrs Bird) one important thing about the system.

All went well until the last day of school before the holidays. That morning, the Bird House was in its usual state of panic. Mrs Bird, of course, took it all in her stride. As usual, she was an Information Service ... a Weather Report ...

... an Answering Machine ...

... a Reference Library ...

. . . a Short Order Cook . . .

. . . and an Early Warning System.

As the door banged shut behind them, Mrs Bird slumped into a chair and mopped her brow. Peace and quiet at last! She liked this time of the morning when she had the house to herself.

Mrs Bird groaned . . . it was Mrs Bates wanting to borrow another cup of sugar. Emily thought that what she really wanted was a good gossip. She was right!

12

This time it was the postman.

Then it was the gasman.

13

The gasman left and the electricity man arrived. He left and a man from the Water Department arrived to inspect the drains. He left and . . . you've guessed it. It just wasn't Mrs Bird's morning . . . someone else arrived!

RRRING!

GOOD MORNING, MADAM! I AM FROM THE *ACE VACUUM CLEANER COMPANY!* I WOULD LIKE TO DEMONSTRATE OUR WONDERFUL, REVOLUTIONARY NEW MODEL THAT CAN SUCK, WASH, BLOW, SWEEP AND CLEAN!

And so, with typical skill and artistry, the trained salesman confidently went about his business.

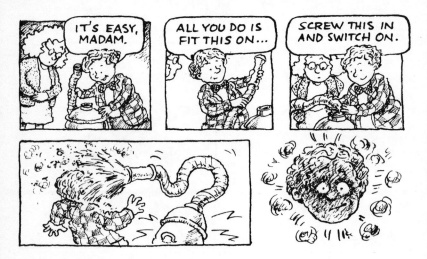

Mrs Bird's patience finally snapped.

So, out came the travel brochures she had got in a mad moment one day as she was passing the travel agent.

After school, Robin, Snoo and Mum pored over the travel brochures while B.B. helped Jay look at a map of the world.

Without wasting a moment, Mrs Bird picked up the phone and dialled SupaSunSational Holidays in the High Street.

Snoo, Robin, Jay and B.B. dashed upstairs.

Out came the sun-glasses, sun-hats and snorkels!

Snoo pretended that they were all in a fashion show modelling beachwear. "Robin," she said in her poshest voice, "is wearing a delightful Hawaiian shirt and striped Bermuda shorts. I have on a pink towelling waistcoat and am carrying a startling fuchsia beach-bag. So chic! Jay is dressed in a blue-and-white designer T-shirt and matching trunks while little B.B.'s ensemble would grace the most elegant salons of Paris . . . a large straw sun-hat, and a yellow-and-red sun-dress set off by a charming bucket and spade!"

Everyone laughed but suddenly the air was shattered by a piercing noise.

To let you see just how bad a Class 1A Emergency really is, here are a few examples of a Class 1B Emergency.

1: A colossal twenty-metres-high monster is loose in the neighbourhood, crushing everything in its path and heading your way.

2: The people next door plan to have a two-week-long Heavy Metal Rock 'n' Roll party through the wall from your bedroom.

3: You arrive at school and remember you have forgotten to do your homework for "killer" Jones the maths teacher. Get the picture?

23

Pinned to the back of the box was a notice. It said: IF THE RED LIGHT IS FLASHING PRESS THE RED BUTTON AT ONCE! DO IT NOW! DO NOT DELAY!

Nothing happened at first . . . then, gradually, a strange whirring noise could be heard.

25

Mrs Bird rushed to the window.

But then . . .   . . . and then . . .

. . . one by one the others joined B.B. in mid-air.

Mrs Bird, floating near the ceiling, quickly opened the book to see if it said anything about the flying kitchen. It did. It was the thing Albert had forgotten to tell her!

Snoo's performance was hardly West-End standard, but then again, she was two metres above the floor at the time!

Suddenly Mrs Bird, now the right way up, gave a sigh of relief.

Mrs Bird turned to the section marked FLIGHT INSTRUCTION.

It worked! Gradually everyone sank to the floor. Relief all round! (Except for B.B. She liked the floating.) Everyone gathered round the kitchen table as Mum read out more of the instructions.

Good question! The answer of course is that they won't! While Mrs Bird and the others tried to figure out what was under the brown blotch, B.B. went over to the sink.

Looking round, Mrs Bird realized that B.B. was going to turn on the wrong tap. She shouted a warning . . .

The kitchen shot off into deepest space at an
incredible speed, hurling everyone across the room.

In the corner, a rather untidy but unhurt heap disentangled itself. Snoo grabbed hold of the sink and managed to pull herself up.

Snoo turned the hot tap/speed control off bit by bit and gradually the kitchen slowed down. Finally, she turned off the tap completely and the kitchen stopped. B.B. jumped up and joined Snoo at the window.

Robin got out his YOUNG PERSON'S GUIDE TO THE GALAXIES and looked in the section marked GREEN PLANETS. He found out that scientists could not agree on what made these planets look green.

Some scientists, for example, thought that the planets were actually blue and yellow but were spinning so fast that it looked as if they were green.

Others thought that they might be giant parks for aliens to play football on, while a very few scientists thought they were made out of mouldy cheese . . . (This last group of scientists was in the five- to six-year-old age range, so I think it's safe to ignore their theory.)

However, no sooner were the words out of her mouth when Snoo, who had been gazing out of the window at nothing in particular, suddenly found herself looking at something very much in particular!

Snoo's simple answer to that was, "NO!"

There was a moment's silence while the rest of the family wondered if this was Snoo acting again. Then all at once they realized she wasn't *that* good and rushed to the window.

The little green traffic warden behaved just like our home-grown variety. (Surprise, surprise!)

Mrs Bird tried to explain that she and her family were strangers in the neighbourhood and didn't know the Intergalactic Traffic regulations. But the little green traffic warden wouldn't listen.

Mrs Bird had learned quite a few lessons in her life. One of the most important was ... THERE IS NO POINT IN ARGUING WITH A TRAFFIC WARDEN. So ...

Snoo turned on the tap and the house jerked like a railway carriage. Then, with a clank and a judder ...

And so, slowly they drifted across the vast reaches of space. The vacuum of the limitless gulf. The infinite abyss. The cold, bleak, dismal vistas. That's right . . .

They were in that part of the universe that's like the local football ground on a wet Saturday afternoon. Then, ten minutes later . . .

B.B. helped Snoo butter the bread while Jay got out the cups and plates and Robin set the table. Mrs Bird made the tea and everyone helped themselves to cheese and pickles. "This is nice," said Emily as they sat round the table. "Just like home."

It certainly was, because just as they had finished . . .

Snoo went to the door.

Mrs Bird had the uneasy feeling that this had happened before!

Ten minutes later, Mrs Krspltx was still there, having a nice long chat.

Which went on . . .   and on!

Eventually, half an hour later . . .

Mrs Bird and the children sat down at the table again to try and figure out what to do. But they didn't get very far with the problem because . . .

and . . .

and again . . .

Glumly, Mrs Bird sat down at the kitchen table. This wasn't the kind of space adventure she'd seen in Flash Gordon!

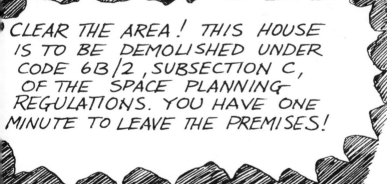

CLEAR THE AREA! THIS HOUSE
IS TO BE DEMOLISHED UNDER
CODE 6B/2, SUBSECTION C,
OF THE SPACE PLANNING
REGULATIONS. YOU HAVE ONE
MINUTE TO LEAVE THE PREMISES!

Mrs Bird sprang into action.

But instead of a roar from the engines, all that was heard was a rather final-sounding . . .

If Mrs Bird had looked in the back of the little book she would have found a simple explanation of what had happened. It was this . . . the inter-ratcheting fulcrum modifier had de-stabilized because the gear-spline protector had become disengaged, causing the central pivoting device to de-activate and confuse the sprocketizer which caused the whole lot to go CLUNK! Clear? No? Don't they teach you anything at school?

48

In other words . . .

But Mum hadn't been to Advanced
Astro-Physical Engineering Classes for nothing . . .

Mrs Bird didn't get a chance to show off her
technical expertise because . . .

Everyone rushed to the window and peered out. Sure enough, in the distance, they could just make out an object rushing towards them. It certainly didn't look like another bulldozer.

"It's not bright enough for a meteor," Mrs Bird muttered. "What could it be?"

"I hope it's not going to crash into US!" said B.B. Everyone was startled. They hadn't thought of that! Jay shaded his eyes and stared hard . . .

Suddenly everyone recognized it at the same time.

The shed cannoned straight into the bulldozer and
they were both smashed to bits. The family stood and
gaped as fragments of garden shed and bulldozer
floated past the kitchen window.

Then, Robin spotted something . . .

A figure carefully disentangled itself from the wreckage and peered round the shattered door.

They rushed to the door as Dad came in.

Mr Bird had always had a low opinion of robots.
    I know this is unfair to all our robot readers but I
do hope you won't write in and complain – that's just
the way he was.

So, five minutes later, when Mr Bird's sore head had been bandaged and he had drunk two cups of hot sweet tea and eaten half a dozen of his favourite curranty biscuits...

Mrs Bird opened the FLIGHT INSTRUCTION MANUAL.

Jay rushed over to the washing-machine and turned the wash-programme dial.

The kitchen's engine burst into life.

The Intergalactic Kitchen executed a perfect flying
turn and rocketed back towards the Earth at an
incredible speed.

If the massed brains at BONCE could not work out
how to make the alien fuel then you can be sure it
must be ultra-super complicated. (I think.)

Just then . . .

The kitchen plunged down through the layers of the Earth's atmosphere. Sparks flew off the roof and there was a sizzling sound as if someone was frying a giant panful of eggs. Luckily, the protective screen was still working, or the kitchen would soon have been like Jay's last attempt at making toast . . . hot and soggy on the inside and charred black on the outside.

The Direction-Finder worked perfectly too and soon they were in sight of home.

The alien spaceship shot straight into the air like a . . . well, like a giant hamburger actually. If you've ever had the misfortune to have had a hamburger thrown at you, then you'll know what I mean.

This was a record for the Bird family as everyone had agreed with Mum in 5.6 seconds. This was lucky, as they really didn't have time to argue.

Two minutes later the kitchen touched down at BONCE and the aliens landed beside it.

All was quiet for a few seconds. Then, with a soft swish and click the door of the alien spaceship opened and out stepped their leader.

At that moment, Mrs Bird appeared in the kitchen porch.

Unfortunately, the alien leader seemed to be lacking in basic politeness.

The alien troops rushed out of the spaceship and formed a ring round the family.

The alien leader came face to face with Mr and Mrs Bird. He glowered at them angrily.

But it seemed as if the alien leader believed this nasty rumour . . . (it's amazing how they spread, isn't it?) . . . because he glowered even more.

But the alien leader remained unconvinced.

Mrs Bird was looking hard at the alien leader.
Somehow he seemed familiar!

Suddenly she grabbed the startled alien leader by the hand and shook it vigorously.

Mr Krspltx stood sheepishly as Mrs Bird introduced him to Albert and the children. As he shook hands with them he began to look more crestfallen and sad.

"I'm delighted to meet you," he said in a choked voice. He pulled out a handkerchief . . . "You are all so nice . . ."

B.B. was off on a rescue mission! She felt sorry for Mr Krspltx and wanted to cheer him up. So she dashed back into the kitchen to get him a present. A few seconds later she reappeared and rushed up to the surprised alien leader.

Mr Krspltx thanked B.B. and took the bottle. As he looked at the contents a slow smile spread over his face. Quickly he unscrewed the top and sniffed. His smile grew wider. He tipped up the bottle, shook some on to his finger and tasted it. His smile became a beam of delight. He hugged B.B. and did a little dance of joy as he shouted to his crew.

IT'S FUEL!

WELL, I'M BLOWED! TOMATO KETCHUP! NO WONDER WE COULDN'T FIGURE IT OUT. IT WAS **TOO SIMPLE!**

The clever experts had obviously thought that because the fuel was for an alien spaceship it had to be very complicated. It just goes to show that sometimes the simple solution to a problem is the best one!

IS THERE MORE OF THIS?

AS MUCH AS YOU NEED. I'LL JUST PHONE THE SUPERMARKET AND ORDER A LORRY-LOAD. I'LL ALSO ORDER FOOD FOR A PARTY.

A PARTY! WHOOPEE!

I WANT TO SET THE TABLE.

And so, when the clever experts had been set free . . .

74

A merry time was had by all. Addresses and photographs were exchanged and promises made to meet again next time the aliens were in the neighbourhood.

Then the ketchup arrived and everybody helped to load it on board.

Soon the fuel tanks were full and Mr Krspltx gave the order to start engines. The aliens waited nervously but as the starter button was pressed . . .

the spaceship's motor burst into life!

The crew waved from the windows and Mr Krspltx said goodbye to the Birds.

Mr Krspltx climbed up the ramp to his spaceship and gave a last wave from the doorway. Everyone cheered.

The door shut silently behind him and the quiet hum of the spaceship motor grew to a loud whine as the ship slowly lifted off. Suddenly it gathered speed and shot into the sky.

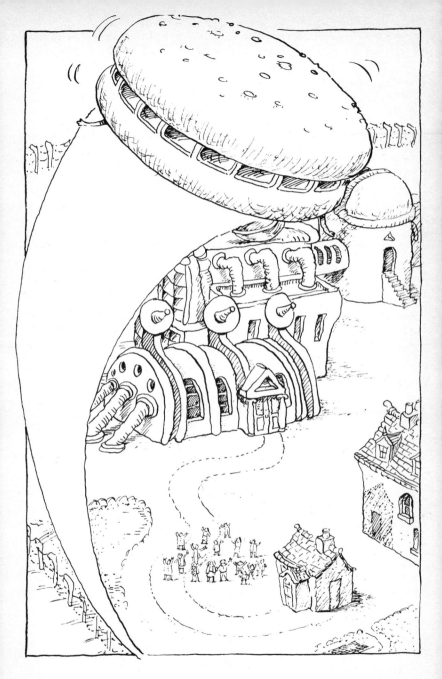

But when Mrs Bird got through to the travel agent
there was a disappointment in store.

This didn't upset Mrs Bird in the least. She hadn't been half-way round the universe to let something like this stop her!

And so, not long afterwards, as the Intergalactic
Kitchen floated gently down towards the Greek
Islands . . .